S0-AYO-000

JUMPING JENNY

This **PJ BOOK** belongs to

_____

_____

PJ Library®

JEWISH BEDTIME STORIES and SONGS

For the two extraordinary Tamars in my life,
both endless sources of inspiration — E.B.

To my little jumpers, my son Riccardo and
my daughter Martina. — R.G.M.

Text copyright © 2011 by Ellen Bari
Illustrations copyright © 2011 Lerner Publishing Group

All rights reserved. International copyright secured. No part of this book may
be reproduced, stored in a retrieval system, or transmitted in any form or by any
means—electronic, mechanical, photocopying, recording, or otherwise—without the
written permission of Lerner Publications Company, except for the inclusion of
brief quotes in an acknowledged review.

KAR-BEN PUBLISHING, INC.
A division of Lerner Publishing Group
241 First Avenue North
Minneapolis, MN 55401 U.S.A.
1-800-4-Karben

Website address: www.karben.com

Library of Congress Cataloging-in-Publication Data

Bari, Ellen.
    Jumping Jenny / by Ellen Bari ; illustrations by Raquel García Maciá.
        p.   cm.
    Summary: Jenny's love of jumping helps raise money during her school's fundraiser.
    ISBN 978-0-7613-5141-2 (lib. bdg. : alk. paper) [1. Jumping—Fiction.]
    I. García Maciá, Raquel, 1975- ill. II. Title.
PZ7.B250376Ju 2011
[E]—dc22   2009030920

Manufactured in China
2-43285-12822-11/2/2016

051728K2/B1045/A6

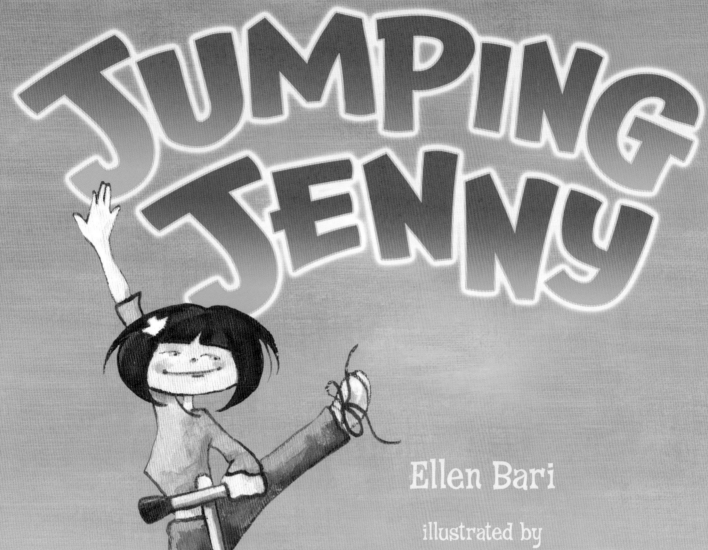

JUMPING JENNY

Ellen Bari

illustrated by

Raquel García Maciá

KAR-BEN
PUBLISHING

Jenny was born to jump.

Nothing made her happier.

Every day on the way home from school, she jumped over the cracks in the sidewalk,

vaulted over fire hydrants,

bounded over hedges, and leaped over Mrs. Fenster's fence.

At home, she grabbed a snack, got on her pogo stick, and jumped some more.

But *some* people didn't think Jenny's jumping was so joyous.

"Jumping is for frogs," scolded Mrs. Jacobs, after Jenny knocked over all the caterpillar bins in the science room. Jenny bit her lip as she cleaned up the mess. Her classmates snickered.

"These cafeteria catastrophes must cease!" announced Ms. Cohen, after Jenny bounced into the hot lunch cart, splattering mashed potatoes in every direction. Ms. Cohen was not smiling as she pointed to the door. Jenny was not smiling as she ate her lunch in the hall.

One afternoon, just as Jenny was about to jump over a fence, a loud chorus of *Ribbit! Ribbit!* suddenly came from behind the hedge. She lost her balance and splashed down into the mud. "Jumping is for frogs," someone shouted. Jenny clenched her teeth to hold back the tears.

That evening at home, a terracotta teapot toppled.

"No more jumping in the house!" Jenny's mother fumed.

"But I love to jump," said Jenny. "One day I'm going to jump to the moon."

"Maybe so," said her mother, "but this house will not be your launch pad."

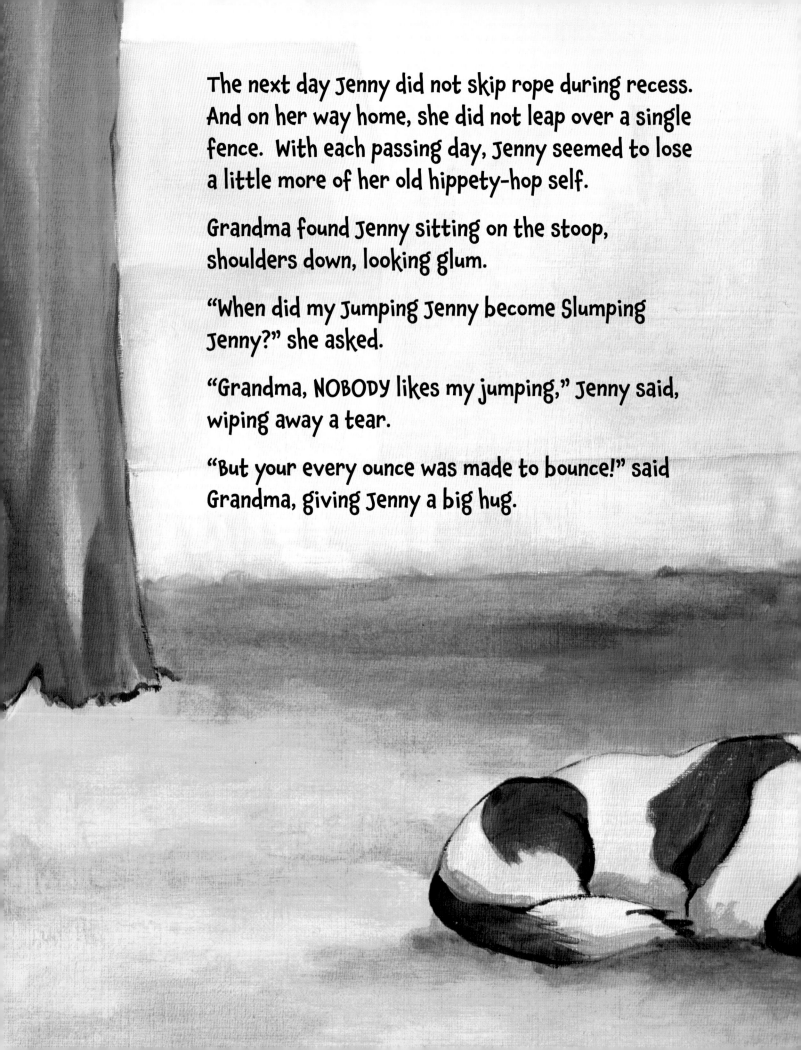

The next day Jenny did not skip rope during recess. And on her way home, she did not leap over a single fence. With each passing day, Jenny seemed to lose a little more of her old hippety-hop self.

Grandma found Jenny sitting on the stoop, shoulders down, looking glum.

"When did my Jumping Jenny become Slumping Jenny?" she asked.

"Grandma, NOBODY likes my jumping," Jenny said, wiping away a tear.

"But your every ounce was made to bounce!" said Grandma, giving Jenny a big hug.

The next day, Jenny's teacher suggested a class *mitzvah* project. "I went to Africa last summer to volunteer at a school in Uganda," she said. "Let's have a fair to learn about African traditions and raise money for the books and computers the Ugandan school needs. Any ideas?"

Jeremy volunteered to teach African drumming, and Monica offered to do tribal face-painting. Tamar would bake and sell African ginger cookies. As her classmates were buzzing with ideas, Jenny was silent.

"I'm not good at anything but jumping," Jenny moped, dragging herself home.

That night she sat on her bed staring at her pogo stick.
After Jenny stopped jumping, she had disguised it with a mop
and an apron. Now it seemed to be talking to her.

She wrote down what she thought the pogo stick
was saying:

Jumpathon
1,000 Jumps

For the first time in days, Jenny smiled. "I'll jump 1,000
jumps! If I can get people to pay for every jump, I can
send lots of books to Uganda."

"The most you've ever done is 250 jumps," her mother warned, when Jenny blurted out her idea.

"I know, Mom," said Jenny. "But, I REALLY want to do this."

To Jenny's surprise, her friends and family pitched right in. They coached her when she jumped (not in the house, of course), and kept a journal of her progress.

Before long, Jenny was a pro. She could even jump backwards with one hand free.

As the day of the fair got closer, Jenny and her friends went door to door asking for pledges.

Aunt Becca pledged a nickel a jump, Uncle Zev promised a dime, and Grandma said she'd pay a quarter for every jump! Before she knew it, the pledges added up to $1 a jump. But could she do 1,000 jumps?

The night before the big event, Jenny could hardly sleep.

When she came to school, the yard had been transformed into an African village. Music was playing and the smell of spices filled the air.

There were long lines at all the booths as children and their parents made beaded necklaces, sampled African foods, and watched a slide show about their sister school in Uganda.

Finally it was time for the Jumpathon. Jenny carried her pogo stick up to the stage, her heart racing.

"1,2,3,4,5..." Jenny's gym teacher, Mr. Kaminsky, started counting.

Jenny was up to 500 jumps when she felt a familiar tickle in her nose that warned her she was about to...

Ah-CHOO!

The crowd held their breath as Jenny took a tissue from her mother, wiped her nose, and kept right on going.

By now everyone was counting,

"...535, 536, 537..."

"...847, 848, 849..."

Gideon brought Jenny some ice water. She gulped it down without missing a jump. Her hands were sweaty and her legs felt wobbly. Then she saw Grandma's face beaming through the crowd.

"You can do it, Jenny!" Grandma yelled.

Jenny swallowed hard, and took another jump, and another, and then another.

"...998, 999...

...1,000!"

"Way to go!" shouted Grandma, as Mr. Kaminksy lifted Jenny onto his shoulders and carried her through the crowd.

"Jumping Jenny!" the crowd cheered.

When Jenny awoke the next morning, she saw her own smiling face on the front page of the local newspaper.

CITY TIMES

Jumping Jenny
Bounces to Her Goal!

CITY TIMES

Ugandan Kids Jump For Joy

And a few months later Jenny was in the newspaper again!

Author's Note

The book is meant to encourage every reader to make a difference in the world. As Jenny learned, you can make this happen while doing something you are passionate about. This story was inspired by a project at the Hannah Senesh Community Day School in Brooklyn, which my daughter attended. One of the dads returned from a research trip to rural Uganda, and reported on the sad state of the schools there. He thought the Hannah Senesh community could make a real difference in the lives of children there by partnering with a Ugandan school. Through a variety of fundraisers, students, teachers and parents have supported the school with clothes, books, computers and money to build desks and replace a roof for safe harvesting of clean rainwater. You can make the world a better place by enlisting the thing you love to do for a good cause. We can all participate in Tikkun Olam, repairing the world, in our own way. —E.B.

Ellen Bari is the author and creator of numerous books, media and exhibits. To some of her childhood friends, her claim to fame is still her audacious 1,000 jumps on a shiny metal pogo stick many years ago! Ellen lives in Brooklyn with her daughter, but the only jumping they do these days is on and off subway cars to "stand clear of the closing doors." Learn more at www.ellenbari.com.

Raquel García Maciá was born in Spain and has a Masters Degree in Illustration from the Istituto Europeo di Design in Rome, Italy. Raquel has twice been awarded first prize at the International Contest of Illustration in Bologna, Italy. She works as an artist in both Italy and Spain, and has illustrated fiction books for children for Belgian, Italian, American and Spanish publishing houses.